The Giant Golden Book of

ELVES AND FAIRIES

with *Assorted Pixies, Mermaids, Brownies, Witches, and Leprechauns*

Selected by JANE WERNER

Pictures by GARTH WILLIAMS

A GOLDEN BOOK · NEW YORK

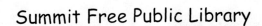

J-nf

CONTENTS

When a Ring's Around the Moon *Mary Jane Carr* 9

Singeli's Silver Slippers *Martha Inez Johnson* 10

Song for a Summer Evening *Mildred Bowers Armstrong* 19

Little People's Market *Dorothy Brown Thompson* 19

A Goblinade *Florence Page Jaques* 20

The Brownie in the Garden *Elsa Ruth Nast* 21

The Second-Hand Shop *Rowena Bennett* 29

Pipes and Drums *Lilian Holmes* 30

The Pixies' Scarf *Alison Uttley* 31

The Fairies *William Allingham* 40

The Cannery Bear *Ray St. Clair* 42

The Bored Goblins *Dorothy Brown Thompson* 48

The Gift *Jane Werner* 48

Halloween Song *Marjorie Barrows* 49

Finding Fairies *Marjorie Barrows* 50

The Lost Merbaby *Margaret and Mary Baker* 51

The Little House *Elizabeth Godley* 61

The Room Beneath the Tree *James Stephens* 62

Where Hidden Treasure Lies *Sheila O'Neill* 66

Ring-a-ring o' Fairies *Madelaine Nightingale* 76

When a Ring's Around the Moon

By Mary Jane Carr

1   The wee folk will be tripping,
      In their silver dancing shoon,
    Ring-around-the-meadow,
      When a ring's around the moon:

2   Curtsy to the right and left,
      And curtsy to the middle—
    The fiddler will be fiddling
      On his tiny fairy fiddle;

3   In and out and round about,
      A magic circle making;
    The pipers will be piping
      Till their tiny throats are aching.

4   Oh, few may watch the wee ones dance,
      For fairy guards are spying,
    And down beneath the grasses
      All the dancers will be hieing;

5   But harken well, what time you see
      A ring around the moon;
    And you will hear the music
      Of the wee folks' dancing tune.

SINGELI'S SILVER SLIPPERS

TRANSLATED FROM THE SWEDISH

By Martha Inez Johnson

Around the cottage in the dim twilight stood the youngest little elves in the forest. They tried to look through the windowpane at Singeli, who sat on a little footstool beside her father, Marten-the-shoemaker. She was sewing rose-pink boots for her rag doll, and was working surprisingly hard at it. Not for a single moment did she look up, so she did not see the curious elves.

Nor did she see the wicked trolls far away at the edge of the forest. The trolls were staring and staring, trying to discover why the elves were watching Singeli.

Marten-the-shoemaker looked up a moment from his work, and rested his eyes on his little daughter's bent head. Very little of this world's goods and riches had he been able to give her. That she might own one lovely thing, one thing of beauty, he had given her a rare name—Singeli.

He rose and stirred the fire on the hearth. The flames flickered, and their light fluttered into the dark corners of the little cottage. Marten-the-shoemaker stood by the fire waiting, as he so often did. He expected that something of all the beauty and happiness in the great world would find its way through his doorway to his little daughter. But Singeli was ten years old, and still the fairy-of-fortune had not shown so much as the points of her silver slippers in the little cottage at the edge of the forest.

Marten softly hummed an old song about a maiden who danced in silver slippers over rose-covered meadows.

"Hm! Rather better than these little cloth boots I am making for my doll," remarked Singeli cheerfully.

Suddenly the door was pulled open, and the shoemaker's wife entered from the goat stable with a pan of milk.

"Are you standing there singing foolish little rhymes?" she asked sourly. "You had better make a pair of wooden shoes for Singeli."

Marten seated himself meekly on his three-legged stool, but when his wife had left the room he pulled out a goatskin that gleamed like silver.

"Singeli," he said, "you shall be as lovely as the maiden in the song. You shall have silver slippers."

"But father," answered Singeli, looking up from her sewing, "you will never be able to finish them. Mother will think it is foolish."

"Even so, I shall make them."

And when Marten-the-shoemaker's wife came into the room again, Marten was busy with the silver slippers.

"Now that is a stupid thing to be doing!" she exclaimed. "Why make such trash for the child when she needs wooden shoes?" But her voice was not stern. It was a marvelous thing to her how much Marten-the-shoemaker loved his little daughter!

When the rose-pink boots for her doll were finished, Singeli said good night to her parents. Her mother, too, tired with the day's work, went to rest. But Marten sat far into the night beside the flickering embers, working at the little silver slippers.

Suddenly there was a knock at the door. Marten-the-shoemaker went to open it, and there stood the fairies-of-fortune on the doorstep. They came into the room in a long line, and they all bent over the half-finished little slippers, stroking the smooth leather with loving hands as they whispered,

"Little slippers,
Go only on bright roads,
Only on good roads,
Only on right roads."

Then the fairies went to the little bed where Singeli lay sleeping in rosy dreams, and said,

"If you, dear child,
Go astray,
Silver slippers
Will vanish away."

All this was seen and heard by the elves, who had slipped into the cottage through the half-open door. They had crept to the very edge of Singeli's little bed; sitting there, they could easily watch the radiant fairies-of-fortune.

But the house-*tomte,* who guards each Swedish home, stood near the door to see that no wicked troll entered. Now and then he let these ugly creatures peep in.

"A father's love will be rewarded," said the fairies one to another, and softly as they had entered they disappeared, with the small, curious elves at their heels and the trolls clumping along behind.

Marten-the-shoemaker brushed his hand over his eyes. Had he been dreaming? But he looked at Singeli's slippers and saw that now they were real silver, as soft as silk.

The slippers were finished by St. Johanne's Eve. That evening the elves were again looking through the windowpanes. But away at the edge of the forest sat the wicked trolls, wondering how they might steal the silver slippers without too much trouble, for they were always lazy fellows.

In the little cottage stood the shoemaker's wife, hands on her hips, marveling at the beautifully finished slippers.

"Now these are a masterpiece!" she said. "But certainly our child can never wear them. Make her a pair of wooden shoes instead."

So Marten-the-shoemaker made his daughter a pair of little wooden shoes. He fitted the little silver slippers to her feet first, and then placed the wooden shoes over them. The elves, the trolls, and the house-*tomte* saw the silver gleaming when Singeli walked, but humans saw only the rough wooden shoes.

Singeli ran over the mountainsides, uphill and downhill. She played with goats and kids. Once in a while she lost her way in the great forest, and naturally she lost the shoes sometimes, even as the fairies had foretold. Then what a search there was, uphill and downhill, in the goats' stables, in the cottage. Often the house-*tomte* came dragging home with them after dark when Singeli had gone to bed with tears on her long, golden lashes.

The years went by, and Singeli grew up. The silvers slippers grew, too, and fitted her as well each year as when Marten-the-shoemaker had made them.

When she was no longer a child, Singeli found work on one of the king's estates in the middle of the great forest. Marten took her there. It was wintertime, and the snow lay like a warm blanket over fields and gardens. Toward evening they saw the lights from the king's court, and in the last turn of the road they passed a whole procession of sleighs. In the most beautiful one reclined the young king, wrapped warmly in a wolf-skin coat and bear-skin blankets. The sleigh bells rang as though for a feast.

"Stop!" cried the young king, but the driver did not stop until they reached the foot of the little hill.

"Wasn't there a gleam as if from silver shoes when that girl went by?" asked the young king.

"I didn't notice," replied the driver.

But the king sent a rider to find out. The messenger soon returned, saying that the girl they had passed wore only wooden shoes.

"Strange," muttered the young king, sinking down among his warm fur robes. "It must have been a shining star that I saw falling in the distance."

There had been a great fox hunt around the king's forest estate, and on this cold winter night the hunters were on their way to the great city where his palace stood. Toward morning all the sleighs had arrived. The king was called at once to sit in parliament.

The wise old counselors asked him to find a queen for the country.

"Yes," answered the young king, smiling, "when I meet a girl who goes as swiftly as the hind to help in sorrow, as lightly as the wind to give joy, and as gently as a breeze in the linden tree."

The wise old counselors shook their heads, and thought the young king was making fun of them.

Meanwhile, at the gateway of the king's estate in the great forest stood Singeli, and waved farewell to Marten-the-shoemaker, who disappeared with dragging steps towards the highway.

"The silver slippers will guide her in the right way," he thought. "Into them I have put all my love for her."

No one on the king's estate ever noticed that the new servant girl wore silver slippers under her wooden shoes—except the house-*tomte*, of course.

The spring came, the cattle had to be driven to the pastures, and Singeli became the herd girl. Singing as she went, she drove the herds before her up the roadway. There was a fragrance of resin in the forest, and back of fallen trees and large stones sat the trolls, peeping at her. Large trolls and small trolls, they all saw the silver slippers under the wooden shoes, and they all wondered how to steal them from her. But the day was bright and the trolls had to keep out of sight. Towards evening, with golden coins and leafy branches twisted in their ugly hair, they clumped up to the gray shepherd's hut with the green thatched roof.

On the step, Singeli had placed her silver slippers, and they shone like two stars. Within the ring of light around them, the trolls dared not come. There they stood, and stretched out their long fingers towards the gleam of silver.

Under the step sat the house-*tomte,* looking out and shaking his little fist at the ugly robbers.

"Don't you dare wake the little one who sleeps alone in the great forest," he whispered.

"We shall not trouble her, if only we may have the slippers," mumbled the trolls.

"Take them!" laughed the house-*tomte.* But the trolls dared not step inside the ring of light around the shoes.

The summer went by quickly. The buttertubs were filled and there were many cheeses, because the little herd girl was diligent and careful. Never had the little herd-hut-*tomte* helped as much as he had this year. And Singeli, wandering far over the pasture-lands, never went astray.

One evening near autumn Singeli sat on the steps of the shepherd's hut, knitting. She had taken off her wooden shoes, and the silver slippers shed a lovely light for a long way.

Strangely enough, not a single troll was to be seen. They were floundering about down in the marsh, laughing at a black horse that would not mind his master. On the back of the horse sat a rider, as pale as the little white elves who watched helplessly. The wicked trolls were pulling bits of turf and reed from under the horse's hoofs, so that the black creature sank deeper into the marsh.

"Ho!" cried the rider, but the only answer was an echo, far, far away in the mountains. They sank deeper and deeper, the dark horse and the proud rider.

Suddenly a swan's cry sounded. Singeli jumped up, dropped her knitting, and ran in the silver slippers down to the marsh where the cry had come from.

The rider heard her footsteps, quick as a hind's, light as the wind, gentle as a breeze in the linden tree. Had angels come to carry him away? No, it was only a herd girl. But she made a loop of the red band she had been knitting. Skipping from one bit of grassy turf to another, she threw the loop over the rider's head. All the little elves of the forest and pasture hurried forward, and with the red band they pulled the rider up from the marshy water to dry ground.

The elves carried him all the way to the step of the shepherd's hut. There he lay all night in a trance. When he awakened, the little herd girl had already driven the cattle out to the pasture. Hunting horns sounded from the forest, and towards the hut came a large group of hunters. They lifted the rider onto one of their horses and rode carefully, slowly, towards the king's estate.

In the evening, when the cows and goats came tinkling through the forests from the pastureland, Singeli looked for the stranger. But all was quiet; no living being was to be seen. Singeli, surprised, drove the cattle into the barn.

"That was an unthankful one!" she said to herself.

After several days, Singeli and her animals left the pastureland for the winter, and she drove her herd towards the village. In the twilight they came to the king's estate. There were lights in all the windows, and inside there was feasting and joy. Cows and sheep came to their usual winter barns, but no one had time for Singeli—at least not at first.

But soon she was called to help. The cook handed her a large plate with newly baked cakes—cream puffs they were—and Singeli in her wooden shoes carried them into the dining hall.

There many young noblemen were seated, and fine ladies. Singeli was so bewildered with all the splendor and richness that she stumbled. The plate fell to the floor, the cakes bobbed like balls around her, the wooden shoes slipped off, and there she stood, wearing her silver slippers.

At that moment the most stately of all the young men arose. It was the young king. As an ornament he wore a red band around his neck.

"Here is one who goes as quickly as the hind, as lightly as the wind, as gently as the breeze in the linden tree," he called.

"She must be a disguised princess. She is wearing silver slippers," everyone whispered.

"She saved my life," went on the young king. All the people bowed before Singeli, because they understood that she and none other would be the queen for whom they longed.

Marten-the-shoemaker often wondered on what roads the silver slippers had led his daughter. One day, when he stood on the step in front of his little cottage, a long, long caravan came towards the little house. At the head rode Singeli, dressed like a queen.

"Have you become a queen, my child?" asked Marten. "Did the silver slippers bring this about?"

"This is the reward of a father's love," replied the young king. "A father's love is like silver slippers, which guide on bright roads, good roads, right roads."

And so the years went by. Good Queen Singeli grew old, but whenever she went in the large kingdom she left a bright road behind her. And when she died all people longed to hear her footsteps again.

After that, whenever the elves in the great kingdom saw a star fall in the evening, they would call out, "See, Queen Singeli has gone by."

But the wicked trolls would run and hide themselves behind fallen trees and large stones.

Song for a Summer Evening

By Mildred Bowers Armstrong

Fireflies in the twilight—
The fairies might be there—
Each with a little winking star
Showing in her hair.
And when the trees are still, and one
Leaf alone is blowing,
Perhaps a pixie flew from it,
Going where he was going.

Little People's Market

By Dorothy Brown Thompson

Come and buy—
Hear my cry—
Elves and fairies, come and buy!
I have cobweb-lace in plenty,
Mushroom-parasols are twenty,
Lady-slippers, fairy-shoon
Fit for dancing in the moon,
Squares of moss for pixie mats,
Hollyhocks for nixie hats,
Acorn-cups for goblin tea—
Won't you come and buy of me?

A Goblinade

By Florence Page Jaques

1 A green hobgoblin,
   Small but quick,
Went out walking
   With a black thorn stick.

2 He was full of mischief,
   Full of glee.
He frightened all
   That he could see.

3 He saw a little maiden
   In a wood.
He looked as fierce as
   A goblin should.

4 He crept by the hedge row,
   He said "Boo!"
"Boo!" laughed the little girl,
   "How are you?"

5 "What!" said the goblin,
   "Aren't you afraid?"
"I think you're funny,"
   Said the maid.

6 "Ha!" said the goblin,
   Sitting down flat.
"You think I'm funny?"
   I don't like that.

7 "I'm very frightening.
   You should flee!"
"You're cunning," she said,
   "As you can be!"

8 Then she laughed again, and
   Went away.
But the goblin stood there
   All that day.

9 A beetle came by, and
   "Well?" it said.
But the goblin only
   Shook his head.

10 "For I am funny,"
   He said to it.
"I thought I was alarming,
   And I'm not a bit.

11 "If I'm amusing,"
   He said to himself,
"I won't be a goblin,
   I'll be an elf!"

12 For a goblin must be a goblin
   All the day,
But an elf need only
   Dance and play."

13 So the little green goblin
   Became an elf.
And he dances all day, and
   He likes himself.

THE BROWNIE IN THE GARDEN

By Elsa Ruth Nast

Bobby liked the new house from the first. It had a look of mystery about it, and of adventure, set as it was deep in an over-grown lawn shaded by great, dark, feathery larch trees. It had a big window in front set with panes of colored glass, and a real tower, and a great stretch of tangle-bushed garden out in back. Bobby liked all that.

It was out at the edge of town, and that seemed fine to Bobby, too. There was lots of space to explore, which appealed to him after the matter-of-factness of a city apartment.

But Bobby had left his playmates behind. He had no one to explore with, no one to clatter with him up the long curving stairs to his big new room, with space for his electric train to be set up all the time and everything. Bobby had no one to play with at all. And that was bad.

Dad was busy in his new office. And Mother was busier than ever making new curtains and drapes and repainting furniture. So Bobby was really on his own.

A pet might help, perhaps, he thought, so he hit upon a plan. He could not ask for a puppy right now, for, as Mother and Daddy had explained to him, there were so many things they had to buy that every dollar had to be stretched three ways and split down the middle before spending.

But kittens, so Bobby had heard, were not so much in demand and often, in fact, wandered about unfed and unclaimed. So each night he left a bowl of milk on the back porch, hoping a stray kitten would find the milk and stay to be his playmate and pet. That was his plan.

It was there the mystery began. Every morning the milk was gone. Yet no sign of a kitten appeared.

21

That was all Bobby noticed at first. But gradually he became aware that toys he had left around the afternoon before he would find neatly put away. And the coat or cap he had dropped on a chair would turn up neatly hung on its own hook.

Bobby's mother noticed this, too, and she was surprised and pleased. She thought her boy was growing up. But Bobby was even more surprised. For he knew he was being no more careful than usual, which was not very careful at all. And he could not imagine who would be doing all this for him.

So he began to watch.

One rainy morning beside the empty milk bowl he found what looked like the damp print of a tiny shoe.

The next morning, behind a pillar on the porch, he found a tiny brown pointed cap. Bobby thought it looked just the size for the owner of that tiny shoe.

So Bobby thought up another plan. That night he crept downstairs when everyone else was fast asleep. And he curled up with a blanket on the back porch swing, close behind the bowl of milk.

He waited and he waited. But the night was ever so still. There were only the crickets chirping and leaves rustling in the breeze. And Bobby's eyelids grew so heavy that at last he fell asleep.

He woke with a start! A small hand was plucking at his sleeve. Quickly Bobby looked down. And there on his knee stood the tiniest little man you could ever wish to see. He had bright black eyes and rosy-brown cheeks. And he was dressed all in brown—tiny suit, neat brown hose, and tiny brown shoes with turned-up toes.

"Why," said Bobby, "who are you?"

"A brownie, of course, as anyone can see."

"Of course," said Bobby. "I'm sorry I didn't know."

Bobby, like most children in these unhappy days, had never seen a brownie. That is not surprising. There are very few around nowadays. And fewer still ever let themselves be seen.

They live just around the corner, where no one thinks to look. They like the back of an old dark closet, or a shadowy attic nook. And they never come out when people are around.

So it was not surprising that Bobby had never seen a brownie. And these days, sad to say, it is not even very surprising that he had never heard of one. So Bobby's eyes were wide as he stared at his new friend.

"You have my cap," said the brownie, with a bright, sharp look in his eye.

"Why, yes," said Bobby. And he pulled from his

pajama pocket the tiny scrap of brown.

"I need it," said the brownie.

"Of course. It's yours."

And Bobby held it out.

The brownie looked surprised.

"Aren't you going to bargain with me?" he asked. But he reached for the cap without delay.

"Bargain?" asked Bobby.

"Yes," the brownie explained. "It's the custom, you know. When a human—that's you—finds something belonging to Little Folk—brownies and such—he asks for a reward before he will give it back. Everyone has done it for hundreds of years."

He had the cap now and was pulling it down over his pointed ears.

"Oh," said Bobby, with a disappointed sigh. "I didn't know, of course. Anyway, I suppose it was you who picked up my toys. I wanted to thank you, and to meet you if I could. Because I've been lonesome here."

"A nice thought," said the brownie, with a nod of his brown head. "And you're a nice boy, I can see. So I'll tell you what I'll do. If you'll say not a word to a soul meanwhile, I'll give you a reward anyway. Not a word, though!"

"Oh, no!" promised Bobby. "I'll be still as a stone."

"Fine," said the brownie, and he gave another nod. "I'll be back tomorrow night, same time, same place. For tomorrow night the moon will be at the full."

What that meant, Bobby had no time to ask. For the brownie was nowhere to be seen.

Well, as you may guess, that next day seemed a hundred days long to Bobby. And his mother could not guess what was the matter with him. He was quiet all day, and she knew he was thinking hard about something.

But night came at last, and bedtime—(hurrah!). And at last the house was quiet, so Bobby could creep downstairs once more and curl himself up in the swing.

And it may be that his eyes did close. For the first thing he knew, that same small hand was plucking at his sleeve. And the full moon was shining in his eyes.

"Come along," said the brownie. "We haven't a minute to lose."

And down the back porch steps he skipped, with Bobby close behind. Straight down the moon-path through the garden they went, back to where the bushes grew so tangled and so thick.

"This way," said the brownie, marching ahead. And Bobby found himself following, through an opening he had never seen, into a clearing that shone with silver light.

Then his eyes grew wide, but he could not make a sound. For that clearing was full of Little Folk!

"Fairies," said the brownie, with a wave of his hand. "It's midsummer's night, you know."

Bobby nodded, though he hadn't known, and followed the brownie along.

"Come meet the Fairy Queen," he said. "If she takes a fancy to you, who knows? You might see Fairyland."

They walked through a pool of silver light to the foot of a leafy throne.

"Good evening, Your Majesty," the brownie said, bowing low. "May I present Bobby, a human friend of mine?"

And Bobby, bowing too, gazed in deep surprise at a wise little face beneath a stardust crown. But the Queen was busy directing the fairy crew, who were making preparations for the ball. She had time for only a smile and a nod in Bobby's direction. "Come back later, young man," she said.

So Bobby bowed again, low as he could, and then he and the brownie walked on.

"Little to the right—no, higher, higher," he heard a piping voice say.

"Hey, watch where you're going!" cried another little voice.

The brownie stopped short, with Bobby at his heels. Just before them loops of spangled cobwebs swooped low between grasses on the left and grasses on the right. And teams of panting pixies were tugging them into place to decorate the fairy dancing ring.

"Sorry to startle you," the pixie spoke again. "But we're in a hurry. The ball starts soon, you know."

"Sorry, nothing!" his team-mate broke in.

"He's only sorry he hasn't time to play a trick on you, human child. That's what pixies mostly do, except on nights like this. Make way, make way!" he suddenly cried, with a great waving of scrawny arms.

Bobby and the brownie jumped aside, as a little man in green went scurrying by. Over one arm was looped the handle of a round iron pot. In the other hand he clutched a tiny shoe.

"Out of my way," he muttered. "Clear the path. Have to get this slipper to the Queen before the ball begins."

"That's the leprechaun," the brownie whispered. "They're the fairy shoemakers, you know. And they always think someone is trying to steal their pots of gold. That's why he was carrying his with him."

"I see someone loitering near the tree root," said Bobby. "He looks as if he might be after gold."

The brownie shielded his eyes with one hand and peered into the shadows.

"Oh, that's a gnome," he said. "They live underground, digging jewels and gold from the rocks with their picks. And they only come up for special occasions like this.

"But here is something else you rarely see. Look farther up the trunk of that tree. See the tiny doorway with someone standing there? It is one of the wood nymphs, who are ever so shy. They live in the deep woods and dress all in green, and they almost never, never are seen."

Then from the clearing they had left came sounds of cricket fiddles tuning up, and bullfrog *chug-a-drums*.

"The ball!" cried the brownie. "The ball has begun!"

So back they raced, and found a place close beside the cobweb-spangled ring. More fairies were arriving

now. They were flying down on beetle-back and dragonflies and such. And their laughter rang out tinkly, like tiny tinkling bells.

Now the beat of the music rose and swelled, and the dancers circled and dipped and swayed. The music reached out into shadowy spots and drew more and still more dancing couples in.

Now shadowy wood nymphs slipped in and out, and grumpy gnomes set down lanterns and picks and tapped out the rhythms with their small heavy boots. The leprechauns laid down their hammers and tacks, and jigged a brisk measure with wee pixie folk.

Such whirlwind of dancing young Bobby had never dreamed of!

"Soon now we'll speak to the Fairy Queen about your visit to Fairyland," the brownie whispered, a-tapping his toe.

But just at that moment, high overhead, a cloud passed over the moon. The little clearing darkened. There was a windy rustle, like a long, sad sigh. And a few fat raindrops spattered on the outspread leaves.

Bobby shivered.

"Come along," he heard the brownie say. And Bobby spied him then through the blackness, waving a firefly lantern round his head.

"Is it over?" asked Bobby.

"Can't do without the moon," said the brownie, as he bustled on.

Just as they reached the edge of the lawn, the tiny lantern flickered, and the brownie was gone.

"Well," said Bobby. "And we never got to speak to the Fairy Queen!"

With a sigh, he tiptoed up to bed alone.

Next morning, before breakfast, he raced to the garden again.

He could not find a hole his size, cleared through the tangle of brush.

But he pushed his way through, though he scratched his face and muddied his hands and knees. And he found the open clearing inside.

There was not a sign remaining of the midsummer ball. Not a trace of fairy folk. Bobby met several sleepy beetles and a drowsy dragonfly, but they paid no attention to him.

Only, where the dancing ring had been, among cobwebs weighted down with dew, a circle of dewy toadstools lifted their sleek round heads.

That was all.

Now Bobby was determined to thank his brownie friend. So he took some spending money and he bought a little car, just brownie size, with a motor and all. And he left it that night beside the bowl of milk.

Next morning, sure enough, it was gone. And in its place was a tiny note, written on a scrap of yellow leaf.

"Thank you," it said, "and good-by." It was signed with a print of the brownie's tiny shoe.

"Good-by!" cried Bobby. "Oh, dear me!"

He ran to his mother with the leaf in his hand. But when he held it out to her, not a trace of a note was to be seen.

Then he told her the story, and she shook her head with a sad little smile.

"If you give a brownie a present he can keep, he must go away," she said. "It's a rule of the Little People, dear. I don't know why."

And she smoothed Bobby's hair with her hand.

It was true, too, it seems. Bobby still put out milk, but the brownie never came again.

One day, though, a kitten came to drink the milk. And a boy and a girl burst through the hedge, looking for their pet. So Bobby found some playmates, and he is not lonely now.

He seldom thinks, these days, about his brownie friend. But once in a while he wakes up in the night with the full moon shining in his face.

And then he remembers. Wouldn't you?

THE SECOND-HAND SHOP

By Rowena Bennett

1 *Down in the grasses*
   Where the grasshoppers hop
   And the katydids quarrel
   And the flutter-moths flop—
   Down in the grasses
   Where the beetle goes "plop,"
   An old withered fairy
   Keeps a second-hand shop.

2 *She sells lost thimbles*
   For fairy milk pails
   And burnt-out matches
   For fence posts and rails.
   She sells stray marbles
   To bowl on the green,
   And bright scattered beads
   For the crown of the queen.

3 *Oh, don't feel badly*
   Over things that you lose
   Like spin tops or whistles
   Or dolls' buckled shoes;
   They may be the things that
   Fairy folk can use,
   For down in the grasses
   Where the grasshoppers hop,
   A withered old fairy
   Keeps a second-hand shop.

The Pixies sought their pixie pipes—
   The Goblins fetched their drums—
The Gnomes and Elves called everywhere,
   "The Pixie Piper comes!"

He led them slowly through the town
   And slowly back again—
Some folks who heard them thought the drums
   Were raindrops on the pane,

And, as the Goblin band drew near,
   Cried, "Listen to the hail!"
(The Goblin drummers chuckled and
   Went drumming down the dale.)

Be careful, pray, the next wet day,
   To make quite sure yourselves,
The patter's really raindrops—not
   The drums of drumming Elves.

Pipes and Drums

By Lilian Holmes

A little Pixie Piper went
   A-piping through the glens;
Some folks who heard him thought his notes
   A robin's or a wren's.

"How late to hear a robin sing,
   It must be nearly ten!"
(The Pixie Piper chuckled and
   Went piping down the glen.)

"It wasn't quite a robin's note,
   I fancy 'twas a wren."
(The Pixie Piper chuckled and
   Went piping down the glen.)

If we'd been there we might have made
   The same mistake ourselves;
The only folks who knew the truth
   Were Goblins, Gnomes, and Elves.

THE PIXIES' SCARF

By Alison Uttley

Once upon a time there was an old woman who went out to pick whortleberries on Dartymoor. She carried a tin can in one hand and a basket in the other, and she meant to fill them both before she returned home.

Behind her came a little boy, her young grandson, Dicky, who had asked her to take him with her across the great windy moor. The old woman's eyes were on the ground, on the low green bushes which spread in a web for miles, but the little boy stared about him at the birds in the air, and the white clouds in the sky, and the great black tors like castles rising from the heather and grass.

"Grandmother, where do those birds come from?" he asked, but Mrs. Bundle shook her head.

"Never mind the birds, Dicky. Pick the worts. There's lots of worts here. 'Tis blue with 'em," and she stooped and gathered the little bloomy whortleberries with her gnarled old fingers, stripping them from the bushes, and dropping them into her can with a rattle like beads falling in a box.

So Dicky turned his head from the blue sky and the flittering birds, and looked at the rounded bushes, like dark-green cushions. Dartymoor was more full of lovely things even than the sky, he thought, as he looked down. He crammed his red mouth with berries, and put a handful in his own little basket. Then he knelt down to look at the scurrying beetles and ants and the long-legged spiders which hurried about their business in the green and scarlet leaves.

Suddenly his attention was caught by a wisp of rainbow color, hanging on a twiggy branch of one of the bushes. He thought at first it was a spider's web, blue and green and gold; but when he picked it up he found it was woven silk, fine as the gossamer sacks which hang in the grasses, shimmering as the dewdrops in the grass.

"What have you got there?" asked old Mrs. Bundle, as she saw him twist the rag round his finger and hold it up to the sun.

"It's a pretty something I've found," said Dicky, going up to her and showing the scrap of silk.

"Drop it, Dicky, drop it! It's maybe something belonging to the Wee Folk."

She lowered her voice to a whisper and looked round as if she expected to see somebody coming.

"It's a pixie-scarf you've found, I reckon," she whispered. "Put it back. It doesn't do to touch their things. They don't like it."

She waited till he dropped the little scarf and then she went on gathering the berries, muttering to herself.

Dicky turned round and looked at the scarf. He couldn't bear to leave it, so he whisked it up again and slipped it in his pocket. Nobody would know, he told himself. He would take it home with him.

He wandered on, picking the ripe berries, following the little old woman, staring and whistling, forgetting the little silken scarf; but as he ruffled the bushes with stained purple hands, and drew aside the tiny leaves, he was surprised to see far more things than he had ever imagined before. Down in the soil he saw the rabbits in their holes, playing and sleeping, or curled in their smooth dwelling houses. He saw the rocks and the little streams and trickles of water flowing underground. Like a mirror was the ground and he watched the hidden life beneath it. Many things were there, deep down, a rusty dagger, a broken sword blade, and he wandered on, staring at the secrets he discovered.

"Grandmother," he called. "See here. Here's something under the grass," but the good old woman saw nothing at all except heather and whortleberries and the short sweet grass.

"Saints preserve us!" she cried, when Dicky scrabbled away the soil and brought up a broken crock of ancient coins. "How did you know they were there?" she asked.

"I seed 'em," said he.

She fingered the money and rubbed it on her torn shirt, but Dicky turned away. He didn't care about it. A new feeling had come to him, and he stood very still, listening, waiting.

The scent of the moor flowed to him, wild thyme and honey and moss in wet places. He could hear the countless bells of the

purple heather ringing like merry church chimes, and the wind in the reeds sang like a harp, whilst the deep, dark bogs sighed and moaned.

"I won't touch these," said old Mrs. Bundle, and she threw the coins away into the bog, but Dicky only laughed, for he heard new music as they fell and were sucked down to the depths. The earth itself seemed to be whispering, and the stream answered back, speaking to the bog and the emerald mosses.

"Get on with your picking," scolded Mrs. Bundle. "You asked me to bring you with me a-worting, and here you are, finding queer things as ought to be hid. Whatever's took you, Dicky Bundle?"

But Dicky's eyes were wide with wonder, and he took no notice of his grandmother. Up in the trees were voices talking, two blackbirds were arguing, and he heard every word they said. A robin called: "Come here! Take no notice of those people below. Come here!" and a tom tit swung on a bough and chattered to its friend, the linnet.

More than that, he could hear the low reedy voices of the worms in the stream's banks, and understand their language as they murmured on and on with placid talk of this and that, and pushed their way among the grasses.

Then came the shrill whisper of fishes in the water, and he leaned over the peaty stream to see who was there. Flat round eyes stared back at him, and the fishes swam under a rock as his shadow fell on them. A king-fisher darted past, and Dicky heard its chuckle of glee as it dived and snatched up a weeping fish.

He would have stayed there all night, crouched on the stream's edge, hearkening to the talk of the creatures, listening to the music of the wild moorland, looking at the hidden life which was visible to his eyes, but his grandmother pulled his arm and shook him.

"Didn't you hear me? Dick Bundle! Come away home. My basket and pail are full to the brim, but you've only got tuthree! Shame on you for a lazy good-for-nothing little boy."

Dicky was bewildered, and he followed her meekly along the road to the cottage down in Widdicombe, listening to the voices all the way.

When they got home his grandmother emptied her fruit into the great brass pan, and soon there was a humming and bubbling as the jam simmered over the fire. Dicky took off his coat and hung it up behind the door, and when the scarf was away from him the little voices of the mice in the wainscot and birds in the garden ceased. The cat purred and he no longer knew what she said. The buzzing flies in the window lost their tiny excited voices; the spider in the corner was dumb.

"It's gone very quiet," said Dicky to his grandmother.

"Quiet? It's the same as usual. You go and fill the kettle and put it on ready for tea. Then wash your hands and face. No wonder you didn't find many berries. You ate 'em all."

Mrs. Bundle was indignant with her grandson, and when the two sat down to their tea, she thought of her son, Dicky's father, away in America, earning his living far from the village he loved. She must bring Dicky up to be a good boy. She sighed and shook her head wearily. It was hard with her old bones to have to deal with a lazy young sky-gazer like Dicky.

"Now you can go out and play," she told Dicky when the meal was finished. "I shall make my jam ready for selling to customers, and maybe we shall get enough money to buy you a pair of shoes, for you sadly need them."

Dicky went out to Widdicombe Green and played at marbles with the other boys. Then Farmer Vinney let him take his brown mare to the stable, and Farmer Deacon asked him to catch a hen that had gone astray. So he was busy with this and that, until the moon came up over the hills and the stars shone in the night sky, and the great tors disappeared in the rising shadows.

Then Dicky went indoors for his supper of bread and milk. He went upstairs to the little room with the crooked beam across the ceiling and he said his prayers and got into his wooden bed. Old Mrs. Bundle came up to look at him and tuck in the clothes.

"Now go to sleep, Dicky. I've brought your jacket upstairs, ready for morning. Go to sleep, and God bless you, my dear."

But Dicky wasn't sleepy at all, and he lay with his eyes wide open staring at the moon over the moor and the tall tower of the church across the Green. After a time he heard a high silvery bell-like voice, calling and calling; as clear and fresh it was, just as if the stars were speaking to one another.

"Dick Bundle! Dick Bundle!" cried the tiny voice. "Give me back the scarf."

"Dick Bundle! Dick Bundle!" echoed a hundred little voices, pealing like a chime of fairy bells, ringing like a field of harebells all swaying in the wind.

Dick sprang out of bed and looked through the window. In a rosebush in the narrow garden below, holding a glow-worm in his hands, sat a little man, and Dicky knew he was a pixie. He saw the little creature's pointed cap, and his thin spindly legs, crossed as he squatted among the roses, and caught the green glint of the pixie's eyes.

Behind were many more pixies, crowds of them, perched on the garden wall, clambering in the flower-beds, running across the grass, each one carrying a glow-worm and calling "Dick Bundle" in its shrill tinkling voice.

"Give us back the scarf," they sang.

"Come and fetch it," called Dick Bundle through the window, and he went to his jacket pocket and took the wisp of rainbow silk and held it dangling at the window.

How beautiful it looked! It was quite different with the moon shining upon it, and it moved like a shimmering fish, and glittered in his hands.

"Oh! Oh! Oh!" sang the pixies. "There it is! There it is! Give it back!"

"Come and fetch it," said Dicky again, for he wanted very much to catch one of the little men.

"We can't come in because you said your prayers," they replied, and others echoed: "Prayers. Prayers. No, we can't come in," and their voices wailed and squeaked.

"You come down to us," invited the first pixie, who seemed to be the leader. "You bring it to us, Dick Bundle."

"No," replied Dick. "I can't do that," and he folded the scarf and drew it through his fingers. "I mustn't go out in the night, or I should catch rheumatics like my grannie."

He looked at his fingers and they were shining with light where the scarf had touched them. Yes, it was too lovely a thing to lose!

"Throw it down to us, Dicky Boy," wheedled the nearest pixie. "It belongs to our Queen, and she has been hunting it all day."

"How did you know it was here?" asked Dicky. "I've never had it out of my pocket until now."

"The birds and the fishes and the rabbits all knew you heard their voices, for you stopped to listen, and no human can understand what the other world says. Only the pixies know. So when they told us a boy had hearkened to their talk as they spoke to one another, and had found old coins lost under the ground, and had bent his head to listen to the heather bells and the gossamer harps in the bushes, then we knew you must have found the scarf. For it gives eyes and ears to those who are blind and deaf."

"I'm not blind or deaf," protested Dicky.

"Yes, you are. You can see nothing without the scarf. Throw it back to us, for you can't keep it. We shall torment you till we get it."

"What will you give me for it?" asked Dicky.

"A carriage and pair," said the pixie.

"Show it to me first," said Dicky.

Then a tiny carriage rolled across the garden path, and it was made out of a cunningly carved walnut shell, drawn by a pair of field mice. The carriage was lined with green moss, and the coachman was a grasshopper with a whip of moonshine.

"I can't get into that," Dick complained. "That's no good to me."

He watched the little carriage bowl along into the shadows.

"What else will you give me?"

"A suit of armor," suggested the pixie.

"Show me first," said Dicky, and he leaned low, expecting to see a grand iron suit like the knights of old wore.

A little man staggered along the wall under the window, carrying a suit of shining armor, and the plates were made of fishes' scales, all blue and silver, and the helmet was adorned with a robin's feather.

"No, I couldn't wear that," said Dicky. "What else have you got?" He twisted the little scarf and waved it before the throng of agitated pixies, who wailed, "Oh! Oh! Oh!" as they gazed at it and held out their skinny arms for it.

"I'll give you a fine dress for your grandmother," said the pixie. He brought out of the rose tree a little crinolined dress made of a hundred rose petals.

"My grannie's too stout for that," laughed Dicky. "What else can you give me?"

The pixies scratched their heads with vexation. They didn't know what to give the great human boy who leaned from the window under the thatched roof. All their belongings were far too small for such a giant, they whispered to one another.

Then one of them had a thought. "A bag of marbles," said he.

Now Dicky was the champion marble player of Widdicombe-on-the-Moor, and he thought if he got some pixie marbles he might be the best player on the whole of Dartymoor.

Surely a pixie marble would capture every other, for there would be magic in it!

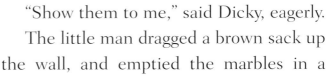

"Show them to me," said Dicky, eagerly.

The little man dragged a brown sack up the wall, and emptied the marbles in a shining pile. Green as grass in April, blood-red, snow-white, and blue as the night sky they shone, each one sparkling in the moonlight.

He held out his hand for the sack, and dropped the scarf from the window, but he took care to grasp the sack before he let the scarf flutter down, for he had heard of the tricky ways of pixies, who outwit humans whenever it is possible. But they were so eager to get their precious scarf, they never even snatched at the bag. With excited happy cries, queer fluting songs, and chuckles like a flock of starlings at evening, they clasped the scarf. Then singing, whistling, shouting, and waving their glow-worms, they ran away, and Dick could see the tiny lights disappear in the distance.

He put the little brown sack under his pillow, and crept into bed, for suddenly he was very tired and sleepy.

The next morning, his grandmother aroused him, and he got ready for school.

"What have you got in that queer bag, Dicky?" asked Mrs. Bundle, as Dicky stuffed it in his pocket. He brought it out reluctantly and showed it to her.

"Don't throw them away, Grannie. They're pixie marbles," said Dick, frightened that he would lose his new possession.

"Pixie marbles? They are pixie rubies and emeralds and I don't know what!" cried his grandmother, holding up the glittering gems to the sunlight.

"You mustn't take them away," said Dicky, sulkily. "I am going to take them to school to play marbles."

"These will buy all of the marbles in the world, Dicky," said Mrs. Bundle. "Now we shall be rich as rich. We will build a neat little house, and have an orchard, and keep a few cows and a horse or two."

"And some pigs?" asked Dicky, quickly.

"Yes, pigs and hens and ducks, too. Yes, all of those and more besides. Perhaps we will have a donkey."

"And a new pair of boots for me and a dress for you, Grannie?" asked Dicky.

"Yes, boots and a dress and a suit of good clothes, my child. Then I will write to your father and bring him home, for we must have him to help with the farm, mustn't we?"

"Yes, oh, yes," shouted Dicky, flinging his arms around her. "And we'll live on Devonshire junket and cream, shall we, Grannie?"

"Maybe we will," she replied. "I think we can manage it."

She trickled the jewels through her fingers, and tried to calculate their worth. Days of poverty were over; she could sit and rest in her old age, and help others, poor as herself. Yes, the pixies had brought fortune to her cottage.

But Dicky Bundle went running off, lest he should be late for school. In his pocket was one of the gems, a smooth round blood-red stone. It made a famous marble, and never missed its aim, so that Dicky became the champion player of all the boys on Dartymoor. That was more important than riches to him, and he took care to tell nobody where his marble came from, lest it, too, should be sold, for money isn't everything.

The Fairies
By William Allingham

Up the airy mountain,
　　Down the rushy glen,
We daren't go a-hunting
　　For fear of little men;
Wee folk, good folk,
　　Trooping all together;
Green jacket, red cap,
　　And white owl's feather!

Down along the rocky shore
　　Some make their home,
They live on crispy pancakes
　　Of yellow tide-foam;
Some in the reeds
　　Of the black mountain lake,
With frogs for their watch-dogs
　　All night awake.

High on the hill-top
　　The old King sits;
He is now so old and gray
　　He's nigh lost his wits.
With a bridge of white mist
　　Columbkill he crosses,
On his stately journeys
　　From Slieveleague to Rosses;
Or going up with music
　　On cold starry nights,
To sup with the Queen
　　Of the gay Northern Lights.

They stole little Bridget
    For seven years long;
When she came down again
    Her friends were all gone.
They took her lightly back,
    Between the night and morrow,
They thought that she was fast asleep,
    But she was dead with sorrow.
They have kept her ever since
    Deep within the lake,
On a bed of flag-leaves,
    Watching till she wake.

By the craggy hill-side,
    Through the mosses bare,
They have planted thorn-trees
    For pleasure here and there.
Is any man so daring
    As dig them up in spite,
He shall find their sharpest thorns
    In his bed at night.

Up the airy mountain,
    Down the rushy glen,
We daren't go a-hunting
    For fear of little men;
Wee folk, good folk,
    Trooping all together;
Green jacket, red cap,
    And white owl's feather!

THE CANNERY BEAR

By Ray St. Clair

Once there was a bear who loved canned salmon. Nothing else tasted good to him—honey, fresh fish, or any of the other things that bears usually eat.

He had tried to get along by helping himself to cans of salmon which the village people kept on their pantry shelves, but he got into trouble too often. Housewives whacked him with broom handles when they caught him, and they usually did catch him because he was too big to get away quietly.

Then, too, his conscience bothered him. He was probably stealing—and besides, he could not get as much canned salmon as he needed.

So he gave this up. He got himself a job in the local salmon cannery where they needed help so badly that they would hire anyone, human or not.

"Now," he thought the first morning, "I am at the place where all the canned salmon comes from. I can get enough for once."

But everybody worked so fast that the bear had no chance to pause for a quiet bite of canned salmon. If he stopped for just a moment his work piled up, and the foreman spoke sharply to him.

He had a hard enough time to keep up with the humans because his new overalls were too tight for him to move freely, and his necktie choked him. He fell behind quite a bit at first until he happened to notice that the humans wore shoes only on their hind feet; so he removed the new shoes from his front paws. This helped, but he still felt discouraged at the end of the day.

As he rode his bicycle home from work that night he thought about his troubles. He ached in every muscle and all four feet were blistered from the shoes. He was so tired that he fell off his bicycle even oftener than usual. His necktie still choked him, but he could not get it off.

Worst of all, he had not been able to get more than five or six cans of salmon. "I wish—," he thought, "I wish—" But he did not know what he wished because he was too tired to think. All he wanted was enough canned salmon, without all this trouble.

He dropped off to sleep as soon as he entered his cave, without even oiling his bicycle or trying once more to get his necktie off.

He dreamed that a little pink bear flitted into his cave.

"Who are you?" he asked.

"I am a fairy bear!" she answered.

"I don't believe it!" he replied. "There is no such thing as a fairy bear, and besides, I'm dreaming!"

"That's right!" she agreed, smiling, "you *are* dreaming, and there *is* no such thing as a fairy bear. But here I am!" She tapped him lightly on each shoulder. "And I am going to grant your dearest wish."

"I still don't believe it," the bear insisted. "But suppose it is true, and you do get me a couple of cases of canned salmon. Will I get into trouble?" He had heard of what happens to people who get their wishes granted.

"Oh, dear no!" she exclaimed. "You are a good bear and you have already earned your wish." With that she vanished and the bear went on sleeping.

Next morning he felt much better. His rest had done him good, and some time during the night his necktie had come loose by itself so he could breathe. Also, though he did not know it, his overalls had split up the back. His shoes still hurt, but no more than could be expected seeing that they were on backwards.

He looked for the cases of canned salmon the fairy had promised, but they were not to be seen. "There is no such thing as fairies or magic!" said the bear firmly, and went off to work.

That day went fairly well. He was able to eat thirteen cans of salmon, hardly a mouthful really, but enough to keep his spirits up. His feet did not hurt too much, but a queer feeling in his shoulders bothered him.

"Lumbago?" he thought. "I must put liniment on them tonight."

So before he went to bed he rubbed his shoulders with some stove oil that a peddler had sold him as powerful liniment. Then he fell asleep.

He dreamed the pink fairy bear flew into his cave again. She wrinkled her nose. "What's that awful smell?" she demanded.

"Liniment," the bear replied. "On my shoulders."

"Liniment nothing!" snapped the fairy bear. "That is common old smelly stove oil. Let me wipe it off." She cleaned him up with a pawful of grass. "What is the matter with your shoulders?" she asked.

"I got lumbago," he explained.

"Don't you worry about those shoulders," the fairy bear said. "They are doing fine!" Then she disappeared.

The bear really felt good next morning, better than he had for weeks. "It must be good luck," he thought, "to dream the same dream twice."

He was so gay that he forgot his bicycle. He skipped and leaped so lightly that his feet scarcely seemed to touch the ground.

Then he noticed that his feet were *not* touching the ground. "It can't be!" he exclaimed—but it was. He was really flying, and he could feel his shoulder muscles working the new wings. They were invisible, so he could not see them, but they were there!

"Wings!" he thought. "What do I want with wings? Who ever heard of a flying bear? I want canned salmon, not wings!" He sat down beside the path to think.

Suddenly the pink fairy bear appeared before him. "Very nice!" She smiled. "A perfect fit."

"I'm dreaming again!" bellowed the bear. "And in broad daylight! This is all very nice indeed, but where's my canned salmon?"

The fairy bear chuckled. "I forgot to tell you about your Radar," she said.

"Never mind the Radar!" exclaimed the bear. "How about my salmon?"

"The Radar is important!" the fairy bear explained. "It is right on top of your head. You know what a Radar is, I suppose?"

"Yes, of course," shouted the bear. "But what about my canned salmon—"

"It works," the fairy bear continued, "just like any other Radar. You won't have any trouble with it." And she vanished.

The bear rubbed his nose. "I'm a flying bear," he wailed, "like nothing anybody ever heard tell of. Besides that, I've got a Radar outfit on top of my head—and nobody ever heard of that *either*." He sighed loudly. "I'm a freak, and my feet still hurt—and all because I wanted a little canned salmon."

Then he remembered that the wings and the Radar were invisible. At least nobody could see that he was a freak. So he went to work after all, and managed to get eleven cans of salmon for his lunch. "I wish," he thought, "that I did not like canned salmon so much. It is such a nuisance working in the cannery!"

As he ate, he listened to the foreman talking to his assistant. "If that fishing fleet won't get here with its load until the morning," he heard the foreman say, "I'll have to send everybody home. If it is only an hour or so out, I'll keep them here. I wish I knew!"

The bear thought for a moment about Radar and wings; then he said slowly, "I think I can find out for you."

The foreman understood enough Bear to follow this. "Go ahead," he said. "I hope you can!"

So the bear climbed the stairs to the roof. Then he flapped his wings and took off toward the sea, working his Radar. As plain as anything he saw the fleet headed in. He could even see the scales on the fish, and he saw that there was a huge catch.

He had to repeat the news several times to the foreman before he could understand the Bear talk, but at last he got the idea. "I don't know how you can be so sure," the foreman said, "with the fleet still two hours out. But I haven't any other information—so I'm going to take a chance on you. I'll keep the workers here, and I'll even put in a call for extra help. For your sake," he added, "I hope you are right."

So for two hours the bear and the foreman paced the floor. Neither said anything, but they were both thinking, and while the foreman chewed his fingernails the bear gnawed his paws.

At last the foreman said, "If you turn out to be right, I will pay you three cases of canned salmon every day to tell me when the fleet will come in and how big the catch is. Maybe you have some kind of instinct."

"I got a Radar," the bear explained.

"I don't understand Bear talk very well yet," said the foreman. "It sounded like something about a Radar. . . ."

And then the fleet arrived, with a huge load of fish, so the foreman did not finish his sentence. Instead, he clapped the bear on the back and shouted, "Here is your salmon, my boy. You did a good job! I'll call a truck to get it home for you."

The bear sighed deeply and grinned all over his face. "That fairy bear!" he thought gratefully.

Aloud he said, "Don't bother."

He pulled a case of canned salmon lovingly toward him.

"I'll eat it here."

The Bored Goblins

By Dorothy Brown Thompson

What do the goblins do
When it isn't Halloween?
How do they spend the whole long year
While no one cares if their ways are queer
Or if their appearance is weird—oh, dear—
I wouldn't be one—would you?

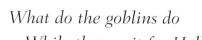

What do the goblins do
While they wait for Halloween?
While the months are tediously creeping by
And no one in all the world asks why
There aren't any goblins about—oh, my—
I wouldn't be one, would you?

What do the goblins do
Until next Halloween?
When never an incantation comes—
No "abracadabras" or "fi-fo-fums"—
Do they just sit twirling their goblin
thumbs?
I wouldn't be one,—would you?

The Gift

By Jane Werner

In the leprecaun's house
On the living room shelf
Stands a small golden box with a key,
And within that wee box,
So he told me himself,
Is a treasure intended for me.

Now I long to stop in
And learn what it may be,
This marvelous treasure he gives,
But the wee man, I guess,
Is forgetful like me,
For he didn't say just where he lives.

Halloween Song

By Marjorie Barrows

Three little witches
   Pranced in the garden,
Three little witches
   Danced from the moon;
One wore a wishing hat,
One held a pussy-cat,
One went a-pitty-pat
   And whispered a tune.

Out flew an owl
   Who glared at the kitten,
Out flew an owl
   Who stared at the rest,
Dancing, with haughty nose,
Each on the others' toes
Down past the pumpkin rows
   Under his nest.

Three little witches
   Blew on their broomsticks,
Three little witches
   Flew to their queen,
Over the windy glen
Into the night . . . But then
They will be back again
   Next Halloween.

Finding Fairies
By Marjorie Barrows

When the winds of March are wakening
  The crocuses and crickets,
Did you ever find a fairy near
  Some budding little thickets,
Straightening her golden wings and
  Combing out her hair?
    She's there!
And when she sees you creeping up
  To get a closer peek,
She tumbles through the daffodils,
  Playing hide-and-seek,
And creeps into the tulips till
  You can't find where she's hid?
    Mine did!

Have you ever, ever come across
  A little toadstool elf
Reading by a firefly lamp
  And laughing to himself,
Or a saucy fairy queen upon
  Her favorite dragonfly?
    So've I!
It's fun to see a fairy flutter
  Off a catkin boat,
And wrap her fairy baby in
  A pussywillow coat;
Oh, don't you love the fairies
  And their fairy babies, too?
    I do!

THE LOST MERBABY

By Margaret and Mary Baker

Once upon a time there were a fisherman and his wife who lived in a little stone house by the sea. It was only a tiny house, but that was no matter, for it was so neat and pretty that no one could wish it to be different. There was a creeper climbing on the wall, and a pot of flowers in each little window; and in the little kitchen there was a tall old clock, and a dresser with rows of blue platters, and there were two chairs and a round table and a carved oak settle, and by the fireside was a wooden cradle.

But the cradle was empty.

"A baby would be so troublesome," said the fisherman's wife. "How should I keep my little house neat and clean with a baby to mind?"

"A baby may be very well in its way," said the fisherman, "but we are happier as we are."

Every day the fisherman set the sails of his boat and went out to sea, and every day his wife went busily about and about the little house. And when her work was done she took her knitting and sat beside the door. She would watch the clouds wandering across the sky, and the waves breaking on the sand, and the sea-gulls wheeling above the cliffs, and then at last she would see the little boat come sailing into the bay, and she would run down to the beach to wave a welcome to the fisherman as soon as he should be near enough to see it.

"Who could be happier than we?" said they.

Now not so very far away there was another little home, but it could not be seen from the fisherman's house however hard one looked, for it lay under the sea. It was only a sandy hollow among the rocks, but it was set about so prettily with sea-weeds that it could not be bettered; and in the hollow lived four little mermaids and a merbaby.

The little mermaids loved the merbaby dearly, but for all that, they often found her a great deal of trouble.

"Oh dear!" they would sigh, "how glad we shall be when she is grown up! She is sure to want us if we swim far away; and see how she plays with our sea-weeds and spoils them, and how she disturbs the sand in our little hollow when we have taken care to make it smooth. She is the most beautiful merbaby that could be," said they, "but she is rather a nuisance sometimes."

Now it happened one day that they found a round basket, such as the fishermen use, floating on the waves.

"Here is the cradle for our baby!" cried they. "When we want to play we can lay her inside and the waves will rock her to sleep."

So they took the basket and stopped up the holes and lined it with sea-weed, and then they put the baby inside. The baby laughed and crowed with delight, and the mermaids swam to their home in the hollow among the rocks. They tidied the sea-weed and smoothed the sand upon the floor, and when they swam back to the cradle and peeped inside the baby was fast asleep.

"See how useful a cradle can be!" they cried. "Now we can swim away to play, for she will not need us for a long, long time."

52

But the little mermaids had forgotten all about the wind and the tide, and while they were gone the basket was carried far away. It was carried so far that at last it came to the foot of the cliffs near the fisherman's house, and there it rolled over and the merbaby slipped into a rock pool among the anemones.

When the fisherman came sailing home he saw something shining at the foot of the cliffs, and as soon as he had brought his boat to land he went to find out what it could be. And it was the merbaby's hair shining like polished gold in the sun.

"Good lack!" cried the fisherman. "What have we here?"

The merbaby was very tired of being all alone and it held out its little arms and cried to be taken up.

What was there left for the fisherman to do but to lift the baby from the pool and hurry home with it as fast as he could?

The fisherman's wife was just as surprised as he. She took the baby in her arms and hushed it and sang to it and coaxed the smile back into its face.

"How it laughs and crows!" cried she. "Look! Its eyes are the color of the sea, and what a dear little tail it has! It is nearly as beautiful as a real baby."

Then she pulled out the wooden cradle and put the baby inside, and there it lay crooning happily to itself. The fisherman's wife kept running to look at it and sing to it, and the baby laughed to see her and tangled its tiny hands in her hair; and the fisherman brought it shells for toys and threaded them in a chain.

That was all well enough, but away under the sea things were not going well at all. The little mermaids had come back from their playing and were looking everywhere for the baby.

"Have you seen our baby?" they asked the plaice who were lying almost buried in the sand.

The largest plaice flicked the sand off itself, for it is not polite to speak to anyone with only your eyes showing. "I have not seen any merbabies for quite a long time," it said, "but that may be because I only see things that are above me on account of my eyes. Perhaps you have noticed my eyes are both on one side of my head," he said proudly, "we are not like other fishes."

"Our baby was in a cradle," explained the little mermaids. "It was only a round basket, but it rocked up and down on the waves and sent her to sleep as well as a real cradle could have done."

"Something that might have been your cradle floated overhead a little while ago," said the plaice. "That is the way it went. Now, if my eyes had been one on each side of my head I should never have seen it."

Away swam the little mermaids, but no sign of the merbaby could they find.

Presently they met a porpoise. "Have you seen our baby?" they asked, and told him all the tale.

"This is very sad business," said the porpoise. "Come with me and we will see what can be done."

So they swam together and asked all the fishes they met for news of the merbaby. Not one of them had seen her, but they were so sorry for the little mermaids that they all joined in the search.

The fisherman stood at the door of his house. "There is no wind," said he. "But look how strangely the sea is tossing!"

How could he know the waves were made by the mermaids and fishes as they looked for the lost baby?

"Let us look for her in the rock pools under the cliffs," said the little mermaids.

The lobsters came out of their holes to see what was wanted.

"We have lost our baby," said the mermaids. "We used to think she was only a nuisance, but now she is lost we are sure we can never be happy until she is found." And they told them all about it.

The lobsters waved their legs in surprise. "How strange to mind losing a baby!" said they. "We never take any notice of our own."

The eldest lobster drew his claws thoughtfully among his feelers. "There is a nasty wicker thing over there that might be your baby's cradle," said he. "It looks too much like a lobster trap for my taste, but as you are not lobsters perhaps you will not mind going near it."

Away went the little mermaids, and among the rocks they found the basket they had used for a cradle. But there was no baby in it.

A big crab came sidling toward them.

"You look as unhappy as though you had just cast your shells," he said. "What can be the matter?"

Then the mermaids told their sorrowful tale all over again and the crab was very sad for them. He went up and down the rock pools explaining what had happened to everything he met, to the fishes and the shrimps and the sea-horses and the whelks, but not one of them could tell him anything.

At last he came to the anemones. "Have you seen the merbaby?" he asked.

"How could we see it?" asked the anemones. "We have no eyes."

"How dreadful to have no eyes!" exclaimed the crab, popping his own in and out with horror at the thought.

"It is not dreadful at all," said the anemones. "We have dozens of feelers and they are much more sensible than eyes, we think."

"But I can't help being sorry for you," said the crab. "Why, even if the mermaids' baby was here you could not see her, and she is worth seeing, they say. Her hair is golden yellow and her eyes are the color of the sea."

"What does it matter what color her hair may be as long as it is hair?" said the biggest anemone crossly. "There is a piece twisted around one of my feelers now and it is most uncomfortable."

The crab brought the mermaids to look. He twiddled his eyes in great excitement. "See what I have found!" cried he.

One of the mermaids gently untangled the hair, and it was so fine and so shining that it could have belonged to no one but a merbaby.

"Our baby has been here," said they, "but where can she be now?"

The puffins came waddling along to see what was the matter. They looked very wise indeed when they heard all there was to be told.

"Now we come to think of it . . ." began one.

"We don't think often, you know," said the others, "but when we do we think to some purpose."

"When we come to think of it," said the first puffin again, "we saw the fisherman pick a merbaby from that very pool where you were talking to the anemones."

"Oh, tell us what he did with her!" cried the little mermaids.

"He took it home, of course," said the puffins. "Your baby is not lost now, because we have told you where she is." And they waddled away.

"Alas!" cried the mermaids. "We are scarcely any better off than when we did not know where to find her. The fisherman's house lies far beyond the reach of the waves and we can go only where the waves can carry us."

Then the mermaids lifted themselves out of the water. "Sea-gulls! Sea-gulls!" they cried. "Fly to the fisherman's house and tell us what has become of our baby."

So the sea-gulls flew across the sand and round and round the fisherman's house.

"Surely there is a storm coming," said the fisherman, "else why should the gulls fly so near and cry so loudly?"

How could he know they had come to see what was done with the merbaby?

"The fisherman has put the baby in the cradle and his wife is tending it as though it was their own," said the sea-gulls when they came back. Then the little mermaids began to weep and sigh. "If they grow to love our baby they will never give her to us again," they sobbed.

"How the sea moans tonight!" said the fisherman. "There is surely a storm coming."

But when the merbaby heard it she began to wail and would not be comforted. "Hush, hush!" soothed the fisherman's wife and ran to pick the baby out of the cradle, but the baby only wailed the more pitifully.

"It is the moaning of the sea that distresses her," said the fisherman's wife. "I could almost weep myself for the sorrowful sound of it." And she shut her window.

How could she know the baby cried because she knew the sound was the mermaids' weeping?

Now, as was only to be expected, the news of the merbaby spread among the fisher-folk, and they one and all made some excuse to come tapping at the fisherman's door.

The fisherman's wife showed the baby proudly. "Look what beautiful eyes she has!" she would say. "And see her tiny hands and the shining of her hair!"

"Yes! Yes!" said the fisherfolk, "but it is a great pity that she has a tail."

"It is a very beautiful tail," said the fisherman's wife. "And there are so many people with feet that to have a tail is to be quite distinguished."

"A tail will be very awkward when she grows up," said the fisherfolk, shaking their heads. "Why don't you put her back in the sea?"

"How cruel that would be!" cried the fisherman's wife. "She is far too tiny to care for herself. Besides, we love her too much to part with her now."

So the merbaby lay from day to day in the wooden cradle and cooed and crooned to itself. The fisherman would leave the mending of his nets to play with it, and his wife sang it gay little songs as she went about her work and ran to kiss its tiny hands and cover it with caresses.

"How could we think a baby was too much trouble!" cried they. "A baby is the loveliest thing in the world."

But the little mermaids in their home among the rocks had no heart to tend the seaweeds, nor to smooth the sand upon the floor and make all neat and tidy; they had no heart to talk to the fishes, nor to play as they had done before.

"How could we think our baby a trouble?" cried they.

"Perhaps some day the fisherman's wife may tire of her," said the eldest.

So every day they swam to the foot of the cliffs. "Sea-gulls! Sea-gulls!" they cried. "Fly away and bring news of our baby!"

And every day the sea-gulls told how the fisherman's wife was fondling the baby as though it were her own.

"Alas! Alas!" wept the little mermaids. "We shall never see our baby again."

And every day when the merbaby heard the sound of their crying it began to wail and would not be comforted.

Then the fisherman would shake his head and ponder. "'Tis strange," said he, "the moaning of the sea is as the sound of someone weeping."

His wife, too, would ponder on the strangeness as she tried to hush the baby's crying, and she pondered so long that in the end she could not help but find the truth.

"Hark!" cried she. "The baby weeps in answer to the sound. It is no moaning of the waves we hear, but the sorrowing of those who have lost her."

Then she lifted the baby from the cradle and kissed it on this cheek and that, and ran with it to the shore. There sat the little mermaids weeping, and when they saw the fisherman's wife they held out their arms.

"Give us our baby!" cried they. "We cannot play nor sing nor be happy till we have her again."

"Sorrow no more. Here is your baby," said the fisherman's wife, and she kissed it over and over and gave it to them.

But when she came back to the little house and saw the empty cradle she fell to weeping as sadly as ever the little mermaids had done.

"It is my turn to sorrow now," said she.

And the fisherman could find no words to comfort her, for he was as sad as she.

But the little mermaids were happier than they had ever been before, and they swam up and down with the baby to tell all the sea-creatures of their good fortune and to thank them for their help.

"You look much happier than you did," said the crabs, but, "It is rather hard to understand family life," said the puffins. "We think a great deal of our babies, but of course they are much nicer than merbabies because they have down and feathers."

"And wings," added the sea-gulls. "We cannot imagine what use arms can be."

The anemones shut up as soon as the mermaids came near. "We are glad you have found the baby, since it pleases you so much," said they. "But do take her away or we shall get her hair all over us again."

The fishes looked at the merbaby very curiously. "Her tail is very fine," they said, "but a fin or two would improve her."

"Or having both her eyes on one side of her head," said the plaice.

"But of course if you are satisfied with her there is nothing more to be said," added the porpoise, and waved his flipper as he swam away.

The little mermaids hugged and kissed their baby. "Fancy thinking she is not perfect!" they cried. "Only the fisherman and his wife know how to love her as we do, and now they are sorrowful because we have taken her back again."

So sometimes they swam to the little bay and called, and the fisherman's wife would hear them and come running to the edge of the sea. Then the mermaids would give her the baby, and she would sit on the rocks to play with it and fondle it.

"It is so lonely now that the cradle is empty," she would sigh for sympathy. "We will come again soon," said they.

But one day when they swam to the bay, though they called and called, the fisherman's wife did not come running out to greet them.

"What can have befallen her?" they asked one another.

Then they lifted themselves out of the water. "Sea-gulls! Sea-gulls!" they cried. "Fly away across the sand and tell us why the fisherman's wife does not hear us calling."

So the sea-gulls flew round and round the little house as they had done before.

"You need not sorrow longer for the loneliness of the fisherman's wife," said they. "There is another baby in the cradle; it has feet instead of a tail, and its eyes are the color of the sky, but she does not seem to mind, nor does the fisherman. They have not heard you call because they are too happy to hear anything but their own joy."

Then the little mermaids swam back to the hollow among the rocks.

"Now we can be happy all day long," said they, "for there is no one left lonely and sorrowing. And some day we will go again to the bay and the fisherman's wife will show us her baby and we will love it next to our own."

The Little House

By Elizabeth Godley

In a great big wood in a great big tree
There's the nicest little house that could
    possibly be.

There's a tiny little knocker on the tiny
    little door,
And a tiny little carpet on the tiny little floor;

There's a tiny little table, and a tiny little bed,
And a tiny little pillow for a tiny weeny head;

A tiny little blanket, and a tiny little sheet,
And a tiny water bottle (hot) for tiny little feet;

A tiny little eiderdown; a tiny little chair;
And a tiny little kettle for the owner (when
    he's there).

In a tiny little larder there's a tiny thermos bottle
For a tiny little greedy man who knows the
    Woods of Pottle.

There's a tiny little peg for a tiny little hat
And a tiny little dog and a tiny, tiny cat.

If you've got a little house
And you keep it spick and span,
Perhaps there'll come to live in it
A tiny little man.
You may not ever see him:
(He is extremely shy):
But if you find a crumpled sheet,
Or pins upon the window seat,
Or see the marks of tiny feet
You'll know the reason why.

THE ROOM BENEATH THE TREE

From THE CROCK OF GOLD by James Stephens

When the children (Seumas Beg and Brigid) leaped into the hole at the foot of the tree they found themselves sliding down a dark, narrow slant which dropped them softly enough into a little room. This room was hollowed out immediately under the tree, and great care had been taken not to disturb any of the roots which ran here and there through the chamber in the strangest criss-cross, twisted fashion. To get across such a place one had to walk round, and jump over, and duck under perpetually. Some of the roots had formed themselves very conveniently into low seats and narrow, uneven tables, and at the bottom all the roots ran into the floor and away again in the direction required by their business. After the clear air outside, this place was very dark to the children's eyes, so that they could not see anything for a few minutes, but after a little time their eyes became accustomed to the semi-obscurity and they were able to see quite well.

The first things they became aware of were six small men who were seated on low roots. They were all dressed in tight green clothes and little leathern aprons, and they wore tall green hats which wobbled when they moved. They were all busily engaged making shoes. One was drawing out wax ends on his knee, another was softening pieces of leather in a bucket of water, another was polishing the instep of a shoe with a piece of curved bone, another was paring down a heel with a short broad-bladed knife, and another was hammering wooden pegs into a sole. He had all the pegs in his mouth, which gave him a wide-faced, jolly expression, and according as a peg was wanted he blew it into his hand and hit it twice with his hammer, and then he blew another peg, and he always blew the peg with the right end uppermost, and never had to hit it more than twice. He was a person well worth watching.

The children had slid down so unexpectedly that they almost forgot their good manners, but as soon as Seumas Beg discovered that he was really in a room he removed his cap and stood up.

"God be with all here," said he.

The Leprecaun who had brought them lifted Brigid from the floor to which amazement still constrained her.

"Sit down on that little root, child of my heart," said he, "and you can knit stockings for us."

"Yes, sir," said Brigid meekly.

The Leprecaun took four knitting needles and a ball of green wool from the top of a high, horizontal root. He had to climb over one, go round three and climb two roots to

get at it, and he did this so easily that it did not seem a bit of trouble. He gave the needles and wool to Brigid Beg.

"Do you know how to turn the heel, Brigid Beg?" said he.

"No, sir," said Brigid.

"Well, I'll show you how when you come to it."

The other six Leprecauns had ceased work and were looking at the children. Seumas turned to them.

"God bless the work," said he politely.

One of the Leprecauns, who had a grey, puckered face and a thin fringe of grey whiskers very far under his chin, then spoke.

"Come over here, Seumas Beg," said he, "and I'll measure you for a pair of shoes. Put your foot up on that root."

The boy did so, and the Leprecaun took the measure of his foot with a wooden rule.

"Now, Brigid Beg, show me your foot," and he measured her also. "They'll be ready for you in the morning."

"Do you never do anything else but make shoes, sir?" said Seumas.

"We do not," replied the Leprecaun, "except when we want new clothes, and then we have to make them, but we grudge every minute spent making anything else except shoes, because that is the proper work for a Leprecaun. In the night time we go about the country into people's houses and we clip little pieces off their money, and so, bit by bit, we get a crock of gold together, because, do you see, a Leprecaun has to have a crock of gold so that if he's captured by men folk he may be able to ransom himself. But that seldom happens, because it's a great disgrace altogether to be captured by a man, and we've practiced so long dodging among the roots here that we can easily get away from them. Of course, now and again we are caught; but men are fools,

and we always escape without having to pay the ransom at all. We wear green clothes because it's the colour of the grass and the leaves, and when we sit down under a bush or lie in the grass they just walk by without noticing us."

"Will you let me see your crock of gold?" said Seumas.

The Leprecaun looked at him fixedly for a moment.

"Do you like griddle bread and milk?" said he.

"I like it well," Seumas answered.

"Then you had better have some," and the Leprecaun took a piece of griddle bread from the shelf and filled two saucers with milk.

While the children were eating, the Leprecauns asked them many questions—

"What time do you get up in the morning?"

"Seven o'clock," replied Seumas.

"And what do you have for breakfast?"

"Stirabout and milk," he replied.

"It's good food," said the Leprecaun. "What do you have for dinner?"

"Potatoes and milk," said Seumas.

"It's not bad at all," said the Leprecaun. "And what do you have for supper?"

Brigid answered this time because her brother's mouth was full.

"Bread and milk, sir," said she.

"There's nothing better," said the Leprecaun.

"And then we go to bed," continued Brigid.

"Why wouldn't you?" said the Leprecaun.

It was at this point the Thin Woman of Inis Magrath knocked on the tree trunk and demanded that the children should be returned to her.

When she had gone away the Leprecauns held a consultation, whereat it was decided that they could not afford to anger the Thin Woman and the Shee of Croghan Conghaile, so they shook hands with the children and bade them goodbye.

The Leprecaun who had enticed them away from home brought them back again, and on parting he begged the children to visit Gort na Cloca Mora whenever they felt inclined.

"There's always a bit of griddle bread or potato cake, and a noggin of milk for a friend," said he.

"You are very kind, sir," replied Seumas, and his sister said the same words.

As the Leprecaun walked away they stood watching him. . . .

WHERE HIDDEN TREASURE LIES

By Sheila O'Neill

Five miles from Limerick, on the road running south toward Cork, stood a little thatched-roof cottage of white stone, with red roses climbing over its tiny porch. Three rooms it had, and four people lived in it: Michael Harrigan, his wife, Molly, and their two children, Colleen and Dennis.

'Twas a merry little family. While the children played under the big oak tree that some folk said was two hundred years old, Molly inside the house sang Irish songs as she spun flax at her wheel or tended the big black pot of stew which hung over the slow peat fire. Michael himself worked for Lord Lester, three miles or so up the road. He whistled "Wearin' of the Green" as he pitched hay down from the big hayloft or bedded the horses for the night.

The Harrigans were happy folk, and kind folk, too. The little house stretched itself until it was big enough to take in every lonely wayfarer.

When the wind blew chill through the branches of the oak tree in the autumn, and the family sat about the hearth, Michael would speak of his brother in America.

"Boston be a long way off," he would sigh. "Could we make money enough, 'tis visitin' him we'd be. Mayhap the little folk will help us."

One night Dennis looked up from where he was making a willow whistle and asked, "What kind of little folk?"

Michael took the yellow-bowled pipe out of his mouth and watched the smoke curl up.

"Well, the fairies are lovely with their dancin' and bringin' kindness to people, but 'tis the leprechaun I'm pinnin' me faith to most. 'Tis he knows where hidden treasure lies."

The next day Dennis looked at the big map on the kitchen wall. He put his finger on it where "Boston" was plainly marked.

"How does one find a leprechaun?" he asked his mother.

"Now the wee folk might not like ye to be searchin' for them. Mayhap they just come when they wish to be seen," said Molly.

But Dennis was not satisfied. He took his old cap from the nail and went out of the house, through the gate, and down the hard white Irish road toward Biddy O'Connor's home. The neighbors said, "Biddy knows the little folks. All goes well wid Biddy." Perhaps she could tell him how to find a leprechaun.

Mrs. Biddy was digging around the roots of her fuchsia bushes just outside her door. She looked up and smiled.

"Is it makin' me a visit ye are?" she asked.

"I'm a-seekin' help from ye," returned Dennis, taking off his cap. "'Tis told that the little folk befriend ye. I have need of the wee ones. I have need of the leprechaun. 'Tis he that finds hidden treasure."

"So—," she spoke gravely. "'Tis that ye would improve your way of living, travel a bit, and eat fine foods at times."

"Indeed, yes," said the boy, "and have a larger house and money in the bank and a trip to the new world where me Uncle Maurice lives. Mayhap a school in Dublin for Colleen and me. Then there are the good neighbors. They could have plenty could I find the treasure."

"Ah," said the good old woman. "'Tis the truth ye speak. Ye would be helpin' the fairies find food and potatoes for all of us. Once," she said softly, "'twas a moonlight night. Two figures went in at me shed a-carryin' somewhat and in the morning there was four sacks of potatoes where two had been before. Ye didn't fool Biddy, lad, neither ye nor Michael."

"We thought ye didn't know," said Dennis, blushing.

"'Tis a good turn I'm owing ye."

Then Biddy bustled into the tiny lean-to kitchen and came back with a pitcher of cold milk and a plate of brown cookies for Dennis.

"'Tis a shoemaker the leprechaun is," she began. "Under the hedges he sits, tappin', tappin' wid his little hammer. He bends over his lapstone and whistles gaily as he works. Small bits of leather lie where he leaves them. Whin he comes back, he picks them up and begins tappin', tappin' again."

"Whose shoes are they?" cried Dennis.

"Fairy shoes, child, to be sure."

"Would he mind if a lad like me were to find him under the hedge? Would he be angry if I caught him?"

"Bless you, no," she said. "But catchin' him is not a-holdin' him. 'Tis slippery like eels they be. Once he gets away there'd be no treasure." She dropped her voice: "That hedge back of the big oak tree—the hedge that runs down to his Lordship's pasture—'tis there I've seen bits of leather, mornings whin I was a-huntin' of me cow."

A moment later Dennis stood on Biddy's doorstep to say good-by. "I am a-promisin'," he said slowly, "that yer good fortune shall come with mine."

The next morning before breakfast Dennis ran out of the kitchen door and then slowly, with careful steps, made his way down toward the pasture hedge. He slipped along the hedge, looking, looking, but finding nothing. Just as he came to a place where the hedge was thickest and bent to the ground, he heard a mournful little tune. He stopped, but the music stopped also. He started walking, and the music began again.

Just before him lay a little cleared spot back under the green hedge. It looked like a place for a child's playhouse, sheltered from the wind and rain. Dennis stopped to look at it, and all the while the music became louder and louder.

"This must be it," he thought. He stooped lower and lower, creeping back into the little cleared place. All at once he saw them—the tiny pieces of brown leather with here and there bits of red, as if for trimmings. But where was the leprechaun?

"'Tis earlier in the mornin' I'll be here tomorrow," he said to himself.

The next morning Dennis slipped out of bed, drew on his old patched blue shirt and trousers, and, walking softly in his bare feet, was gone while the rest were sleeping.

Down past the big oak he went and came again to the hedge row. The music began ringing in his ears. This time he did not stop but went straight down the hedge to the place of the little closed clearing. His heart almost choked him with its beating, for there, with his back toward Dennis, sat the leprechaun. There were the green coat and shorts and white stockings, the little red cap and the red shoes with great silver buckles. The Old One was whistling "Shawn O'Farrell." He whistled, and tapped and tapped with his tiny hammer on the fairy shoe on his lapstone.

Now Dennis had carried something with him that morning. He had caught up his mother's brown shawl from the chair where she had left it lying.

Without even snapping a twig beneath his bare feet, he crept upon the leprechaun.

The Old One turned his head on one side and listened, but he did not turn around. Dennis waited. Presently the Old One turned back to his cobbling and began whistling his merry tune. Dennis spread the shawl carefully and counted the distance. Then with a spring he threw the shawl about the plump little body. Closing in, he doubled it again and again. The Old One struggled, but Dennis caught him tightly against his own body and held him fast.

"Uncover me head," cried the leprechaun sharply.

"Fair enough," said Dennis, "but it's not escapin' ye'll be."

With his free hand he turned down the shawl until the round, wrinkled little face with its twinkling black eyes looked up at him.

"'Tis too tight ye are holdin' me!" insisted the Old One.

"Not so," said Dennis. "'Tis yer trick to get loose."

"Well, well," chuckled the leprechaun. "What is it ye wish?"

"Treasure," cried Dennis eagerly. "Treasure to give me family good livin', and Colleen and me good schoolin', and to take a trip across to the new world, and to buy warm clothes and good food for our poor neighbors."

"'Tis a long, dangerous journey ye'll be goin'." The black eyes looked hard at Dennis.

"Which way?" Dennis asked.

"Where thy horse stands croppin' the grass," the Old One directed.

As they approached the pasture gate, the old man cried out, "Look at me, Dennis!"

Dennis looked, and there was nothing there. No wrinkled round face, no black eyes, no little red cap—nothing. He almost dropped his burden. Then he straightened himself and cried hotly, "'Tis shape ye still have. I can feel ye. And 'tis weight ye have, too. I still have ye."

The Old One chuckled until his body shook against Dennis' chest, but he said nothing until they came to where the mare stood.

"How far have ye been from home, Dennis?" asked the leprechaun.

"Ten miles," answered Dennis proudly.

The old man chuckled again. "Hold me down to the mare's feet," said he.

"No, see here," began Dennis, "'tis no harm ye shall do to this mare. 'Tis our only horse to pull the jauntin' car into Limerick."

"Tut, tut, she'll be croppin' the grass in the mornin'. Come on, boy."

Dennis, stopping, held the leprechaun while the tiny hands rubbed Doll's hoofs gently—first the front ones and then the back ones. Doll stood as if bewitched, snorting a bit but never moving a leg.

Then Dennis stood up and looked at the mare. Her black coat shone in the rising sun. On her back was a silver-mounted bridle, finer by far than Lord Lester's horse wore at the county fair. On her back was a red leather saddle with silver stirrups. Dennis rubbed his eyes with his one free hand.

"Come! Come!" cried the Old One. "The treasure waits!"

At the word "treasure," Dennis came back to himself. With one foot in the stirrup he swung himself, leprechaun and all, into the saddle. Doll's feet began to move. They skimmed the earth. The pasture gate, the house, the old oak, and Lord Lester's castle all disappeared behind them. Strange country spread out on either side, with houses, barns, and fields with men working.

"Are you afraid?" asked the Old One.

"Yes," choked Dennis.

"Will ye go home?"

"Not till I get the treasure," Dennis answered.

Just then, at a turn in the road, Dennis saw before him a deep-looking blue lake. It sparkled in the sun. Dennis shut his eyes. It was well he did so, for just then Doll's movements beneath him seemed different. With a gentle, rocking motion she was moving rapidly.

"She's flying," thought Dennis. For one moment he wished he were home. This was worse than any tale of little folk he had ever heard. He kept his eyes closed until the motion changed beneath him.

Then he saw green fields again, and cattle and men digging potatoes and building fences of stone. On and on they went, miles and miles from home.

At last the Old One spoke again. "Will ye go home?" he asked.

"Not empty-handed," said Dennis.

"Then here we go!" said the leprechaun. Now they were facing suddenly a great, rough mountainside. The road went no farther. Doll stopped and stood waiting.

The Old One leaned forward in Dennis' arms and spoke strange words, magic words.

With a terrible ripping noise a great crack opened at the bottom of the mountain. It ran swiftly upward, tearing out rocks and dirt. Doll snorted and leaped backward.

Dennis shut his eyes again. When he opened them, Doll had begun to move. The crack in the mountainside was larger now. Dennis' hands shook, but he held the Old One tighter. Doll was moving rapidly inside the tunnel. It was light enough to see the trail, but there was no hint of daylight ahead.

"Ye are almost out, lad." There was kindness in the little man's voice.

"He's beginning to like me," thought Dennis.

Suddenly they were on a hard-beaten road again. Dennis, looking ahead, could see the gray turrets of a castle rising behind a high stone wall.

In a flash, Doll stopped, snorting, before a beautiful, tall, carved gate of green copper. Out of the leprechaun's mouth, magic words came tumbling. The tall gate quivered as if shaken by the north wind. Slowly, slowly it began opening, and Doll passed through it.

"Journey's end!" chuckled the leprechaun. "In an empty castle the treasure lies!"

"It's not stealin' I am from any man!" cried Dennis. "'Tis honest treasure I want, treasure found in a cave or buried by a river. This is a Lord's castle."

"Such a lad," the Old One smiled. "This castle is on no man's map. 'Tis here today; 'tis gone tonight."

Presently Dennis found himself going down a long, dark hallway. At the right he turned without the Old One's saying a word and went down a steep flight of steps into a vault. At one side stood a huge, brass-bound chest with open lid.

Dennis' feet would hardly carry him, but he walked slowly until he stood, looking down. He looked and looked and looked. The chest was filled to the top with Spanish doubloons, and with rare jewels, pearls and rubies and diamonds and some necklaces of a rare blue stone. At one side of the chest lay heavy, stout sacks, looking as if the treasure had been emptied from them.

"Is that enough for ye?" chuckled the leprechaun.

Tears stood in Dennis' eyes.

"Oh, sir," he said. "I cannot fill the sacks, for I dare not let ye go. Besides, they are too heavy for me to lift and Doll could not carry them. Why did ye let me see them? They mean so much to poor folk like us."

"So they do. So they do," agreed the little man. He scratched his left ear as if thinking. "I promise ye the treasure," he said at last.

Then Dennis was climbing the dark stairway.

"Surely," he thought, "if the Old One can touch Doll's feet with magic, and open mountains and gates and doors, there is nothing he cannot do."

It seemed but a moment that they traveled back across the countryside. There were no lakes, no mountains this time. Dennis could not speak, and the leprechaun was silent. At the gate of the pasture, Dennis slipped off Doll's back.

He glanced toward the house. His father was just coming out of the kitchen door. He turned and called back to someone inside.

"Sure, and he's all right. He's just slipped off to fish in the river."

Dennis shouted, "Feyther!" but Michael did not even look at him.

"Hush," said the Old One. "'Tis not time yet. Let's watch him find the treasure."

While Dennis stood staring at his father, Michael's feet began to move toward the haystack. Presently he broke into a run.

"Michael," called Molly from the doorway. "Michael, what ails ye? Why do ye run? Where are ye going?"

"I don't know!" Michael shouted back to her. Just then he reached the haystack and stumbled over something.

Molly came running down the path with Colleen close behind her. Michael stood looking stupidly at the heavy sack he had pulled away from the stack.

"Cut the string, Michael," cried his wife.

Reaching behind him, he took his knife from his trousers pocket and with trembling hands cut the heavy cord that bound the top of the sack. He looked down and made some kind of a sound in his throat. The three of them, Michael and Molly and Colleen, looked in silence at the gold and rubies and pearls and the rare blue stones in that sack.

After a moment or so Michael turned to the edge of the haystack and there he saw the edge of another sack. One by one he pulled them from their hiding places until four large sacks stood side by side. Tears were rolling down Molly's cheeks. Colleen held tightly to her mother.

"'Tis the leprechaun did it," said Michael.

"He knows where hidden treasure lies."

He took off his old gray hat and stood uncovered.

"Thank ye, sir," he said, "wherever ye be."

"Put me down, lad," cried a hoarse little voice behind them. Michael and Molly and Colleen turned to stare in amazement at the little man with the green coat, the white stockings, and the little red cap.

"Here's your lad, Michael," he said, smiling all over his round little face. "'Tis a great journey he's been a-makin'. Never once would he give up till he found the treasure."

"Oh, Dennis!" cried Molly. Colleen and Michael crowded close. But Dennis could not say words yet.

"Oh, sir," cried Molly, turning, "I forgot to thank ye." But Molly was talking to the empty air, for the leprechaun had vanished.

Ring-a-ring o' Fairies

By Madelaine Nightingale

Ring-a-ring o' fairies,
Pixies, sprites, and elves,
Dancing with a little boy
As nimble as themselves,
Charm a sleepy song-thrush
To sing a fairy tune;
Was ever such a pretty dance
Seen beneath the moon?